THE FAIRY RACE

The Friendship Fairy Club BOOK 1

To Breana
Tyler, Rylan &
Gysalyn

Follow your
dreams!
♡
Angie
Schnuerle

WRITTEN BY Angie Schnuerle

ILLUSTRATED BY Tami Boyce

ISBN: 978-0-578-75789-6

Schnuerle Publishing
Bonners Ferry, Idaho

TABLE OF CONTENTS

This book is dedicated to my family and friends for pushing me to be brave and share my book with the world. There were times when the butterflies in my stomach were out of control, but you guys stood by me and urged me on. Thank you.

Chapter 1

THE DREAM

The view of Pyrola from the queen's balcony in the top of the cottonwood tree was spectacular this first early morning of Fall. The leaves of the currant bushes were tinged with red and the cottonwoods were turning yellow. The air was so crisp that it instantly woke up your eyes and your nose to the sights and smells of the day.

Princess Balsamfera, Fera to her friends, stood on the edge of the balcony and watched as the kingdom woke up. Puffs of smoke rose from chimneys. Fairies were emerging from their houses to begin their day of work. Birds were chirping their good morning songs.

It was Fera's favorite time of year. She leaned her body against the balcony. Her long black hair touched her forearms. Her wings twitched in the cold. Her blue eyes took in every detail of the kingdom that morning, but her thoughts were already moving to the dream she had that night.

There was an idea that took form in her dreams last night and it was the reason she was awake so early this morning. She had dreamed of a race. A race that had never been done before. She immediately began planning Pyrola's First Fall Race in her head.

The race would have fairies taking off from the area under the queen's balcony in the Royal Cottonwood, flying through the forest, trailing fingers through the icy stream, surfing on a falling leaf, flying under and around the eagle's nest, and back to the Royal Cottonwood.

Now came the hard part: convincing her mother and father (the queen and king) to allow her to organize it. She needed help coming up with a persuasive plan. Time to get the Friendship Fairy Club together.

Fera went to the ladybug plant. She tied notes around the necks of four of the ladybugs and sent them out to her friends. The notes said:

I need help coming up with a plan for a fantastic race. Meet me at the clubhouse at 9:00.

Fera

Promptly at 8:55 the fairies began to arrive. First to arrive was Chloe. She landed gracefully on the moss-covered log and waltzed into the clubhouse. The lamp inside caught the subtle highlights of blond in her short curly brown hair. "What kind of race?" she asked Fera as soon as she saw her.

"Wait for the others to arrive," Fera giggled.

Next came the twins, Tom and Ted. Their blond heads nodded to the girls as they came through the hole. "Good morning Fera. Your note was delivered a little early this morning. We had to get up earlier than usual and race to get our chores done in time," said Tom. Ted nodded.

"I know you boys need your beauty rest, but I've been up for hours and I need help," Fera replied.

Angelina's short blond-haired head popped in. Followed shortly by Daniel's red head. Now the members of the Friendship Fairy Club were ready to begin. They sat down at the table and gave Fera their attention.

"Okay. Last night I had a dream about a fantastic race for Fall. It seemed so real," she closed her eyes as she described her dream. "I saw a hundred fairies flying through trees, over the icy stream, on a falling leaf, and around the eagle's nest. It was so amazing." Fera looked around at her friends.

"Wow. That sounds amazing! I love it," said Angelina.

"Me too, but around the eagle's nest? I don't see your parents allowing that, Fera," stated Ted.

"I agree. That eagle is mean. Remember the time she chased us into this log. She never left until Dr. Panex came with a stick of devil's club," reminded Tom.

"Now I want to organize this race and make it happen, but how do I convince my parents?" ended Fera.

"What if we tried a practice run?" whispered Chloe.

"What?" The other fairies replied.

"Well, if we tried it out and things were fine, that might help persuade Fera's parents," argued Chloe.

"True. Maybe we could distract the eagle somehow?" said Tom.

The friends took a moment to think of what would distract the eagle. She mostly just liked terrifying the fairies that lived there.

"I know! We could let her think there are some fish down by the bend in the river," suggested Daniel. "I could tell the chickadees. You know how quickly they get around. The news could be to the eagle in no time."

"Great idea," said Fera. "Let's try it. Daniel, you tell the chickadees. Then meet us on my mother's balcony so we can watch the eagle's nest.

Chapter 2

ON THE BALCONY

"I love the view from here. Your mother is so lucky," whispered Angelina as her blue eyes scanned the village below. The rest of the Friendship Fairy Club looked out towards the eagle's nest.

"Look! The eagle is getting ready to take off!" Daniel cried. "Now, how will this work?"

"Okay. We'll fly through the trees by the rabbit warren. They are all tipped over and it would be more challenging. Then low over the icy water of the stream. Maybe low enough that we have to touch the water." Fera's brown eyes narrowed as she hesitated. "The leaf part won't work because the leaves aren't ready to fall yet, but we could jump on a few. Then we'll fly around the eagle's nest and back here. What do you think?" Fera looked into her friend's eyes and saw the challenge there.

They were ready. They nodded their heads. "Follow me!" yelled Fera as she dove off the balcony.

The others quickly followed after her. Since this was a test run and they weren't really sure how it would go, they followed Fera. First, they dodged the crisscrossed branches of the trees that had fallen over the rabbit warren. It was trickier than it looked because they were going a little faster than normal. Fera realized that a race through them could be dangerous.

Then they flew down toward the stream and dipped their fingers in as they flew over. The cool water was refreshing. They were getting hot already. Fera led the way to the top of the trees and they all jumped four or five times on the leaves at the top. Next came the eagle's nest. She still wasn't anywhere in sight, so they quickly flew around her nest and then back to Fera's mother's balcony.

They leaned on the balcony and tried to catch their breath. Quick spurts of steam came out of their mouths.

Finally, Daniel said, "That! Was! Awesome! I can't wait to do it again."

"I think it might be easy to ask your mom to let you have this race. It was our first time and it was fast, fun and not too dangerous," added Tom.

"But, the rabbit warren could be dangerous. We weren't going race-fast. If we were racing that fast, we could have hit one of those branches. And luckily for us, the eagle was gone. We might not be as lucky the next time," warned Angelina.

Fera looked at Angelina. "You're right. I was thinking it could be dangerous, too. We will have to do something about the rabbit warren. I'll talk to the rabbits and see if we could make a track through there somehow. And Daniel's trick with the chickadees seemed to work out well. We'll just do it again when the race comes up."

"Let's go get our chores done, think about what we can do to make this work, and meet back at the clubhouse after dinner to discuss this a little more," suggested Chloe.

"Okay," said the twins. "See you later," they smiled as they launched off the balcony.

"We'll work this out, Fera. Don't worry about it," said Angelina. "Chloe, do you want to come by the house? Mom has some spruce soup to give your mom. Is she feeling any better?"

"Yeah. Dr. Panex says she just needs to rest a few more days. It means I have a few more chores to do, but she said that when she feels better, I'll get a break from my chores as well. Your mother's soup has given her more energy. Let's go. See you later Fera!" Chloe said as she and Angelina took off.

"Daniel, thank the chickadees for me, will you?" asked Fera.

Daniel grinned. "Sure. It was fun. I'd better get going." And he flew off as well.

Chapter 3

CHORES

The Friendship Fairy Club members went about doing their chores for the day. While they worked they thought about how they could make sure the race would happen.

Angelina was collecting more spruce needles for her mother's famous soups. Those soups had helped a lot of fairies. Maybe food should be a part of this race? She thought about that. While she was sweeping the floors, her mother started a fresh batch of soup. She kept close by since there was a secret ingredient and so far she hadn't figured it out yet. She finished her chores early and decided to go and help Chloe since she realized that she missed the secret ingredient again.

Chloe had finished cleaning the house, fed her mother some of the spruce needle soup, and heated up the food the neighbors had sent over for her brother and sister. Her father was a messenger fairy and wouldn't be back until dinner time.

When Angelina showed up, they went out to collect seeds for her mother to grind into flour for the bread she made for the village. Angelina shared her idea of incorporating food into the fall race. Chloe nodded thinking that it was a way her mother could repay everyone for their kindness during her sickness. Maybe she could make bread as a prize?

Tom and Ted needed to go in search of late blooming fireweed flowers. Their parents were making fireweed honey, a specialty of theirs. As they flew, they discussed the trick they played on the eagle. "I can't believe it was so easy," they laughed as they flew. They finished early and decided to go and see if Daniel needed help.

Daniel had the hardest chore of everyone. He was picking currants, a lot of currants. They were for the punch his parents made for special celebrations in the kingdom throughout the year. They had a lot to make so that there would be enough for all of the celebrations until next summer when the currants were ripe again. Daniel appreciated Tom and Ted's help.

As they worked, they talked about the leaf part of the race. How could they make that part more fair? Maybe some fairy helpers could be on the lowest branch of the farthest cottonwood. They could hand each participant a leaf that they had to ride to the ground. They would bring that idea to the meeting that night.

Fera, being a princess, still had chores to do. She made sure the ladybug plant had enough aphids, she trimmed the leaves away from the windows of the house and met with Dr. Panex at his house at the bottom of the devil's club bush.

Dr. Panex must have been at least a hundred years old. White tufts of hair stuck out of his ears but there was not a single hair on his head. She needed to pick up her father's sleeping tonic. As she waited for Dr. Panex to make it, she told him about her race idea.

"I don't know if your mother and father will allow you to do that. It sounds dangerous, Fera," Dr. Panex shook his head. "There were only 6 of

you this morning. Imagine over a hundred fairies doing it at the same time. Someone could get hurt."

After her talk with Dr. Panex, Fera decided to meet with the rabbits. She told them her idea. They thought it would be fun to watch and showed her where she could move, bend, or break some branches to make that part safer. "Thanks. I'll keep you updated," Fera said as she flew back home.

Elsewhere in the forest, the chickadees were chatting about the trick they helped play on the eagle. The eagle, not finding any fish in the bend of the river, was flying overhead. She did not look happy.

Chapter 4

BACK AT THE FRIENDSHIP FAIRY CLUBHOUSE

"So, here is what I have been doing about the Fall Fairy Race," Fera started the meeting. "I met with Dr. Panex and he was talking about how dangerous it would be especially with over a hundred fairies flying through it. Makes sense. So, I went and talked to the rabbits. They showed me a place where we could make enough space for a large group of fairies to fly through without getting hurt."

"You told Dr. Panex?" asked Chloe. "I hope he doesn't go to your parents before we do." She chewed her thumbnail as she sent a worried look to her friends.

"Maybe we should make another practice run tomorrow. This time making it a real race. Then we will know if it will work. What do you think?" asked Daniel.

"Good idea," agreed Tom.

"Yeah, it would give us a good feeling about whether it will work or not. More evidence for your parents," added Ted.

"You guys are forgetting about the eagle," reminded Angelina. Her toe tapping nervously.

"Don't worry. We'll just have the chickadees help us again. They enjoyed it this morning.

That eagle is just as mean to them," said Daniel with a wink.

Tom nodded at Ted and said, "We have been thinking about the leaf part. It may not be fair if the lower leaves are taken or you land on one that doesn't fall."

Ted added, "So what if there were fairies on one of the branches handing out leaves to fairies as they come through? We could surf to the ground and then head to the eagle's nest."

"Okay. Let's do it. Let's go and work on the rabbit warren now, so it looks safer to my parents when we race through it tomorrow. Then we can meet on my mother's balcony at 9:00 tomorrow morning. I'll have them meet us there to see the practice run."

When Fera got home, she approached her parents. "Mom. Dad. I need to talk to you." They turned and gave her their attention. "I would like to put together a race for the Fall. My friends and I have been talking about it and we would like you to come and watch it tomorrow morning. Before you say no, please come and watch us. Then we can discuss it after our practice. 9:00. On the balcony. Please. Please. Please," Fera said in one breath.

Her parents took a minute or two to think about it. Fera stood there nervously looking from her mom to her dad. They looked at each other and nodded. "Well, Fera, it seems you have it planned out. We'll meet you on the balcony at 9:00, watch your race, and discuss it when you're finished," stated her mother.

"It sounds fun. Something new for the kingdom. Great idea, Fera," her father said jovially.

"Thank you. Thank you. Thank you," she said energetically as she hugged her parents.

Chapter 5

THE PRACTICE RACE

The next morning everyone was assembled on the balcony. King and Queen Populus sat in their royal chairs to watch the race. Fera and her friends were on the edge of the balcony ready to go. Then the king said, "On your mark. Get Set. Go!"

The fairies jumped off and began the race toward the rabbit warren. At first Fera was in front, since she was the most familiar with the route. Then Daniel flew by and led them through the fallen logs of the rabbit warren. "Hurry up!" he shouted as he dipped his fingers in the water of the stream. Tom and Ted added a burst of speed as they tried to catch up. "Let's go, slow pokes!" he laughed. He leapt from leaf to leaf in the top of the tree. He found one loose one and surfed gently to the ground. Then he sped off for the eagle's nest without a backwards look at his friends.

The rest of the Friendship Fairy Club looked at each other with stunned expressions. This was not what they expected from their friend. "You guys are losers!" he yelled as he flew around the eagle's nest and back to the balcony.

The King and Queen were standing and clapping when all of the fairies finally finished the race. "That was splendid. But how did you know the eagle was not in her nest? It wouldn't be safe to have this race with her there," said the queen.

Daniel, still breathing heavily said, "I had the chickadees lie to her about where some fish were. We'll do it again on the day of the race."

The king laughed, "Good idea, she's always chasing those chickadees, too. I bet they loved that."

"I hope she doesn't find out that it was you guys that lied to her. She won't be happy," stated the queen with a frown.

"So, can we have the race?" Fera asked.

"I think it is a great idea. Let's start making up posters. What will the winner get?" inquired the king.

"Oh. We hadn't gotten to that part. We were just concerned about convincing you to let us have the race," said Chloe.

"I know. Chloe and I were talking about using food during the race. We can have a special feast for the winner, and they can eat with King and Queen Populus at the royal table," suggested Angelina.

"That sounds lovely," beamed the queen.

"The Fall Fairy Race is a reality! I can't believe it. We need to work on the posters and the entry paperwork. Oh! There is so much work to be done," Fera's wings fluttered excitedly as she danced around the balcony.

"Well, we'll leave you kids to work on the details. Make sure I see things before you send them out," her mother commanded as she and the king left the balcony.

"Wow. Did you see me go? I have never flown so fast in my life." Daniel beamed.

"That was great flying," the twins said.

"I mean, really, did you see me? I blew past all of you like you were standing still," Daniel continued.

"We were doing our best," reminded Chloe.

"Yeah, but I won. You guys need to get practicing if you want to beat me." And still Daniel was congratulating himself. His friends just looked at him. "What?"

"You're being rude," admonished Angelina.

"Why? Because I beat you? It was a race. That is the idea. To win. I won. You're just jealous." He looked at his friends. They said nothing. "I have to go." As Daniel flew off, his friends watched him fly away and looked at each other sadly.

"Let's not worry about him right now. He'll come around later. Let's get busy on this race," Fera rallied the others and walked inside.

And the eagle quietly flew out of the Royal Cottonwood Tree. Her mind was on revenge.

Chapter 6

WORKING ON THE RACE

The next two weeks were a whirlwind. The air got chillier. The leaves began losing more of their green tint and were taking on the colors of Fall. The club members, minus Daniel, were busy making posters, finding volunteers, looking at entrance paperwork, and planning the Fall Fairy Race Winner's Feast as well as doing their regular chores.

As Fera and her friends were working, Pyrola was busier than ever. Every fairy in the kingdom was coming to watch a participant that they knew in the race. The feast was being prepared, seating in the cottonwoods was being built, and the course was cleared up to make it safer. The eagle's nest was watched to let racers know when it was safe to practice. Racers flew through the course alone, with partners, or groups. Fairies of every age were leaf surfing. (That was the best thing about Fall. The leaves came off the trees easily and the fairies loved surfing on them until they reached the ground.) Pyrola was happy. Laughter rang in the air.

Finally, the day of the race dawned. The forest was beautiful. Fall had arrived. Yellows, oranges, browns, and reds were everywhere you looked. Smoke was drifting out of chimneys earlier than usual this morning. Everyone was getting ready for race day. Fairies were baking, singing, and stretching before the sun came up.

Fera was on the balcony again. Thinking. What had Daniel been up to for the past two weeks? Where had he been? How could he not have come by to help? Every time one of the others asked those questions, she redirected them with tasks that needed to be done. But it had been bothering her, too.

As if on cue, Daniel flew up. "Hey. Just wanted to let you know that the eagle has been taken care of," he said as he began to fly away again.

"Wait. Where have you been? We could have used your help," said Fera.

"I've been practicing for the race. I am going to fly by everybody. You'll see," he said proudly.

"Is that all you care about? Winning? What about helping your friends?" asked Fera. She pointed to the kingdom below her. "We could have used your help."

"My friends should be happy that I am going to win. See you later, Fera," he huffed and flew off.

"Great," Fera mumbled to herself. "Now what?" Fera continued to look out over Pyrola. What could she do about Daniel? "Maybe I'll go ask Dr. Panex. He always knows what to do." Fera flew off to the devil's club bush. The leaves were yellow and the red berries at the top beautiful, but she still made sure to be careful of the thorns. "Why does he live here? I'll never understand it." She said shaking her head. She knocked on his door. Dr. Panex, still in his nightgown and robe, answered the door.

"A little early for visitors, isn't it?" he asked grumpily. "Come in. Come in. Want some tea?"

"No, thank you. I'm looking for some advice." Fera walked around the room as she talked. "Our friend, Daniel, has been acting so strange lately. He won our practice race, bragged about it, hurt everybody's feelings in the Friendship Fairy Club, and hasn't helped a bit with the work to get the race together. And just now, he said that if we were his good friends, we would want him to do well in the race. I don't know what to do about him. We have missed having him around." She stopped in front of him and looked at him as her eyes filled with tears. "What do I do to get my friend back?"

"Well, Fera, I can help heal the body, but emotions are not my thing. Maybe you should take your problem to the Rosa Sisterhood. They are much better at this than I am," suggested Dr. Panex.

"Who?" asked Fera.

"The Rosa Sisterhood. They keep to themselves, but they are very wise. They seldom come out, but they have their ways of helping. Go to the rose bush on the east side of the village. There is a bench there. Sit down and say what you just said to me. If they have any ideas, they will get them to you," explained Dr. Panex.

"Okay. I'll try anything." Fera sighed. "Thanks. See you at the race later."

Fera arrived at the rosebush. The leaves were burgundy, and a few had settled on the bench. They were cushiony she learned as she sat down on them. Fera began talking. She said everything she had just told Dr. Panex. "I need some help," she finished. Then she sat there and waited. A dark red leaf drifted down and landed in her lap. And waited. Another leaf fell. And waited.

Finally, she stood up to leave. Then she heard a faint female voice. "Wait. The time to fix your friendship is coming. Time heals. Pay attention to the signs and you will know when to heal your friendship." The voice stopped. There was nothing more. Fera looked around. She could not figure out where the voice was coming from. It sounded as if it was only in her head.

"Okay, you're hearing voices, Fera. Great. One more thing to worry about." And she flew back home to get ready for the race.

Chapter 7

THE FALL FAIRY RACE

The banners flapped in the breeze. King and Queen Populus were standing on the Queen's balcony. One hundred sixteen fairies were below the balcony ready to begin racing. Hundreds more were in the trees waiting to cheer on their racers. Six fairies, Fera, Chloe, Angelina, Tom, Ted, and Daniel, were in the group of racers ready to begin.

"Good Luck." They said to each other. Except for Daniel of course. He was looking up at the balcony eager for the race to begin. His friends sighed. What could they do?

The king was looking at the eagle watchmen. When they signaled that the eagle was gone, he yelled, "On your mark. Get set. Go!" One hundred sixteen fairies took off. Hundreds of fairy voices rang through the air shouting encouragement.

The racing group started out so crowded that the racers barely had room to stretch their wings. By the time they got to the rabbit warren, it had thinned out. The Friendship Fairy Club stayed together at first to stay safe. Then Daniel zoomed ahead. He was in the first group to make it through the rabbit warren. The others could see him as he flew down to the water and lightly skimmed his fingers through the water in the stream. Next was the leaf surfing. He reached one of the leaf volunteers first, grabbed his leaf, and took off. It was trickier to do when you had other surfers to watch for.

Daniel was in the lead. His grin lit up his face. It was the best day of his life. His leaf touched the ground and he zoomed towards the eagle's nest. As he came around the back of the eagle's nest, he saw her diving toward him. She reached out with one sharp-taloned foot. He quickly dodged to the right and flew into a bunch of leaves. He was going so fast that he couldn't really see where he was going.

He could hear the eagle slicing through the leaves after him. That was all he could hear. That and the incredible beat of his heart. He wasn't going to make it. He pumped his wings faster until they were a blur. Coming out of the leaves, he saw a woodpecker hole in the tree in front of him. He pushed himself to go faster. He was getting so tired, but to slow down meant death. The eagle was snapping her beak right behind him.

Snap. Snap. Whomp! Daniel hit the back of the woodpecker hole. It wasn't very deep. He jumped up and hugged his body as close to the back wall as he could. The eagle perched right outside. She stuck her beak in, but it wasn't long enough. "Think you could make a fool out of me, did you?" she screeched.

Panting, he replied, "What are you talking about?"

"The chickadees and the fish!" she shrieked.

"Oh, no!" he thought. "I'm sorry! I'm sorry!" he cried.

The eagle started tearing at the opening with her talons. The hole was getting larger. Any second now, she would be able to grab him. Tears began running down his face. Who would save him? Not the Friendship Fairy Club. Not after

how he had treated them lately. "Why was I being such a jerk?" he asked himself.

Just then, the eagle stopped clawing at the opening. She shrieked again so loudly that it echoed in his hole. Then she took off. She left. Why? Daniel still held close to the back wall. What if it was a trick? He heard her screech again, but farther away this time. What was going on? He was too scared to look.

Just then, Ted and Tom peeked their blond heads in. "Are you okay?" they asked.

Daniel closed his eyes, sighed, and nodded his head.

The other Friendship Fairy Club members looked in as well. "It's safe now. You can come out Daniel," whispered Angelina. She reached her hand out to him. He grabbed it and walked out into the sunshine. His eyes immediately began searching the sky.

Understanding what he was looking for, Fera said, "Dr. Panex started a small fire in the eagle's tree. She is over in her nest protecting her babies now."

They could see Dr. Panex signaling them to go back to the Queen's balcony. There was still some smoke in the tree. He would make sure it smoked a little longer to keep the eagle there. Then he'd make sure the fire went out completely.

"Who won the race?" asked Daniel.

"Nobody. Everyone started diving for cover when the eagle came out," said Angelina.

"I'm sorry. I ruined your race, Fera," Daniel said looking forlorn.

"You didn't ruin the race. The eagle did. We should have known that she'd figure it out. She may be mean, but she is smart." Fera said with a shrug. "Next year we'll look for a safer route for the Fall Fairy Race."

The Friendship Fairy Club flew close to the ground and closely together the entire way back to the balcony. The king and queen as well as all of their parents were gathered there. Hugs were given to all of them. Then they were shaken and told never to scare their parents like that again. Everyone headed off to the Fall Fairy Race Winner's feast. Everyone, except for the Friendship Fairy club members. They headed to the Clubhouse.

Chapter 8

BACK AT THE FRIENDSHIP FAIRY CLUBHOUSE

"I am so sorry, you guys," Daniel said as he looked around at his friends. There were still tear stains streaking down his face. "Thank you for helping me. I guess I let the competition get ahead of our friendship."

"We knew you were still our friend. Of course, we would come to help you," Chloe said with a small smile and a shake of her curly brown-haired head.

"I don't know what I would have done if that eagle had gotten you," Fera said, a tear slipping down her face.

"How did you act so fast?"

"We were on the leaves when we saw you charging through the leaves with the eagle on your heels," explained Ted.

"Then Dr. Panex was there. That man shows up in the strangest places. Anyway, he had a plan. We flew close to the ground to the eagle's tree," added Ted.

"We could have flown straight there. That eagle wasn't looking for anyone else. She really wanted to eat you, Daniel," said Angelina.

Fera spoke up next. "Then Dr. Panex started his small fire. We walked to the bottom of the tree you were in. Dangerous by the way. Wood chunks were showering down on us from her trying to get to you."

"We needed to be sure she was going to stay in her tree, so we watched for Dr. Panex's signal. Then we flew up to get you. End of story," explained Chloe.

"We owe Dr. Panex again," Angelina said. "What should we do to show him how thankful we are?"

"Let's go ask my parents. They are at the Fall Fairy Race Winner's Feast. Maybe we could give him some recognition there?" suggested Fera.

The Friendship Fairy Club flew off to attend the feast. They were surprised by what they saw when they got there. Dr. Panex, red to the tips of his hairy ears was being toasted by the entire kingdom for his heroism.

"I guess we don't have to ask your parents. They came up with an idea already," stated Daniel. "I need to thank him as well." Daniel flew up to the platform and walked up to Dr. Panex. Tears filled his eyes once more. "Dr. Panex, thank you so much for saving my life. If you ever need anything, I will do it." He threw his arms around him. Dr. Panex patted him on the back and whispered, "I'd like to not be the center of attention anymore."

Daniel signaled to his friends. They encircled him in a hug, lifted him off the platform, and returned him to his devil's club bush. Daniel's parents had followed with a tray of food for him to enjoy. With Dr. Panex comfortably eating in his own space, the others returned to the feast.

"The race wasn't really a success, Fera, but it was still an adventure. Now what?" asked Tom.

"Ignore him. Let life return to normal for a bit, will you?" interjected Ted.

"Well, I had an idea of a Winter Festival Contest...," said Angelina.

All eyes turned to her. She smiled. A twinkle lit her eyes.

COMING SOON:

THE WINTER CARNIVAL

The Friendship Fairy Club BOOK 2

Made in the USA
Monee, IL
20 June 2022

98044527R00033